Esme
the Ice Cream
Fairy

To all ice cream lovers everywhere

Special thanks to
Sue Mongredien

ORCHARD BOOKS
338 Euston Road, London NW1 3BH
Orchard Books Australia
Level 17/207 Kent Street, Sydney, NSW 2000
A Paperback Original

First published in 2013 by Orchard Books

HiT entertainment

A CIP catalogue record for this book is available
from the British Library.

ISBN 978 1 40832 497 4

3 5 7 9 10 8 6 4 2

Printed in Great Britain

The paper and board used in this paperback are natural recyclable
products made from wood grown in sustainable forests. The
manufacturing processes conform to the environmental regulations
of the country of origin.

Orchard Books is a division of Hachette Children's Books,
an Hachette UK company

www.hachette.co.uk

Esme
the Ice Cream Fairy

by Daisy Meadows

ORCHARD

www.rainbowmagic.co.uk

The Fairyland Palace

Candy Land

Goblins' ice cream van

Market St

Charlie's ice cream

Kirsty's Hou

Wetherbury Village

Jack Frost's Spell

I have a plan to cause some strife
And use those fairies to change my life.
I'm going to take their charms away
And make my dreams come true today!

I'll build a castle made of sweets,
And spoil the fairies' silly treats.
I just don't care how much they whine,
Their cakes and lollies will be mine!

Contents

Ice Cream Emergency

"Bye, Aunt Harri," said Kirsty Tate, hugging her auntie. "It was really nice to see you again."

"Thanks for all the sweets," added Rachel Walker, Kirsty's best friend. She was staying with Kirsty over half-term.

Aunt Harri smiled at them. "My pleasure," she said. "I'm sorry they weren't as nice as normal though."

Kirsty's aunt had the best job in the world: she worked at *Candy Land*, the sweet factory just outside Wetherbury village. She'd come to have lunch with the Tates that day, bringing a big bag of *Candy Land* sweets for everyone with her. Unfortunately, the sweets had tasted terrible. Something had gone badly wrong!

The girls were disappointed but their dismay had quickly turned to excitement when their friend Honey the Sweet Fairy magically appeared in Kirsty's bedroom. She told them that strange things had been happening at her Fairyland sweet factory, and asked if they'd help her.

Kirsty and Rachel hadn't hesitated for a second. Of course they'd help – they loved going to Fairyland! And so, just moments later, they'd been swept up in another wonderful fairy adventure, this time with Honey and her team of Sweet Fairies. It had been the most perfect start to the half-term week, thought Rachel, smiling to herself.

The girls, Aunt Harri and Kirsty's mum were now standing outside Tracy Twist's sweet shop in Wetherbury High Street, where Aunt Harri was catching the bus back to work.

"I hope everything's working properly at *Candy Land* again," she said. "Still, at least the lollipops were nice."

"The lollipops were *delicious*," Kirsty replied, with a secret wink at Rachel. Earlier, the two of them had  met Lottie the Lollipop Fairy, and had a thrilling time tracking down her magic lollipop charm which had been stolen by naughty Jack Frost. Lottie used her magic charm to make lollies everywhere lickably lovely and while it was missing, they had tasted horrible. Luckily, Kirsty and Rachel had helped Lottie get it back, and now all the lollipops in the world were yummier than ever.

"Good," Aunt Harri said. "Well, I've left a special surprise for you back at your house which I hope you like too. Ah, here comes my bus. Goodbye, all of you. Thanks for a lovely lunch!"

"Bye!" chorused Kirsty, Rachel and Mrs Tate, waving to Aunt Harri as the bus drove away.

"I wonder what the surprise is," Kirsty said, when the bus was out of sight.

"Knowing Aunt Harri it'll be something good," Mrs Tate said with a smile.

Rachel smiled too and felt a fluttery feeling inside at the thought of a surprise waiting for them. Whenever she and Kirsty got together, life was always full of surprises!

They headed back towards Kirsty's house and as they walked through the market square, Rachel found herself looking out for more fairies.

Honey had a team of seven Sweet Fairies who helped her create delicious treats, using their special magic charms. Unfortunately, Jack Frost had decided that he wanted all their yummy sweets for himself, so that he could build a gigantic Candy Castle. He had ordered his goblin servants to steal the magical objects, so he could make the best sweets ever. Unfortunately, while the magic charms were away from their fairy owners, sweets and treats didn't look or taste anywhere near as good as usual!

Even worse, this had happened just before the fairies' annual Treat Day – the day when Queen Titania and King Oberon gave every fairy a basket full of sweets. It looked as if those baskets would remain empty unless the girls could help the Sweet Fairies get their magic objects back from the goblins.

Kirsty was scanning the market stalls closely too. "Mum, could we look around, please?" she asked. "We can meet you at home later, if that's okay."

The Tates only lived a few streets away, and it was a safe walk back.

"That's fine," Mrs Tate said, and took her purse from her handbag. "Here," she went on. "Let me give you some spending money, just in case you see something you like."

"Thank you," Rachel said.

"We'll be back in an hour," Kirsty promised.

The two girls said goodbye and made their way through the square. It was

lined with all sorts of different stalls,
selling jewellery, toys, local vegetables
and brightly coloured candles. Then they
spotted an ice cream van, and Kirsty
licked her lips. It was a sunny day, and
she really fancied a tasty, cool ice cream.

"They look nice," Rachel said, looking
at the poster board propped up near the
van. "Caramel Crunch – mmm, my
favourite."

"Chocolate Swirl sounds good too," Kirsty said, her tummy rumbling. "Ooh, and Mint Choc Chip. How will we decide?"

The man in the van smiled. He was wearing a white uniform and hat, and had a badge with 'Charlie' printed on it.

"Would you like to try a few flavours?" he asked. "It might help you make your minds up."

"Yes, please," both girls replied.

"No problem," said Charlie. He gave them each a tiny spoonful of Strawberries and Cream flavour, then another of Mint Choc Chip.

Kirsty put the pink strawberry ice cream in her mouth, expecting it to dissolve deliciously on her tongue. Instead, it felt like a flavourless lump of ice. "Oh!" she said in dismay.

Rachel was about to try the Mint Choc Chip but before she had even put the spoon to her lips, the ice cream had melted to liquid and dripped onto the ground. Strange!

A horrible thought occurred to both girls at the same time. "This must be down to Jack Frost!" Kirsty whispered. "He's even ruining ice cream!"

Enter Esme!

Another customer approached the ice cream van just then and began giving Charlie a long, complicated order, so Kirsty and Rachel seized the chance to slip away.

"Let's look around the van," Rachel suggested in a low voice. "We might see another of the Sweet Fairies."

"Good idea!" Kirsty agreed, feeling
a flutter of excitement at the thought.
Another fairy adventure in the same day
would be a real treat!

The girls searched eagerly around the
van, hoping to see a telltale glimmer or
sparkle which would mean a fairy was
nearby. But even though they looked
at every bit of the vehicle, from top to
bottom and back to front, they saw
nothing unusual.

They wandered around the front of the van again where the customer was just leaving. His hands were now full of ice creams, none of which looked very tasty.

"Goodness!" Charlie exclaimed. "That's cleaned me right out of Chocolate Chunk. Give me a minute, girls, I'll just pop into the back to get some more."

Charlie vanished into the depths of the van and the girls stood waiting at the counter.

"I'm not sure I actually *want* an ice cream now," Rachel whispered. "Shall we go somewhere else?"

Kirsty was just about to agree when

her eye was caught by a spare paper hat on the counter, like the one Charlie was wearing. "Look!" she hissed. "That hat! It's glowing!"

Rachel's eyes widened in excitement and she carefully lifted the hat. Then she beamed as a tiny fairy fluttered out and landed on a stack of cornets, her feet dangling over the edge.

The fairy had long black hair, and wore a pastel-striped top, bright yellow trousers and pink baseball boots. The stripes on her top reminded Rachel of Raspberry Ripple ice cream!

"Hello there," said the fairy in a high, lilting voice. "I'm Esme the Ice Cream Fairy, we met earlier."

"Hello again, Esme. I'm Kirsty, and this is Rachel," Kirsty reminded her.

25

"And we're really glad to see you," Rachel said. She checked Charlie wasn't back before adding, "The ice cream from this van is *awful*!"

Esme nodded, looking serious. "It isn't very nice, is it?" she agreed. "And it's all because Jack Frost took my magic ice cream cone charm. I've got a feeling that the goblins are somewhere in this market with it – would you mind helping me look?"

"Mind? Not a bit!" Kirsty said eagerly. "We'd love to!"

"Here we go," Charlie said just then, reappearing with a large tub of chocolate ice cream in his arms. He opened the freezer lid and slotted it inside. While his head was hidden in the freezer, Esme leapt off the cornet and fluttered into Rachel's skirt pocket. She felt warm and tickly there.

Charlie lifted his head looking confused. "That's strange," he said. "All my ice cream seems to have melted. How could that have happened?"

"Oh dear," Rachel said.

"I'm sorry, girls," he went on. "Maybe this freezer is broken. I'm afraid I'll have to close up while I investigate."

"Thanks anyway," Kirsty said. "I hope you can sort it out soon." She glanced at Rachel as they turned away. "I hope *we* can sort it out, more like," she added in a whisper.

Esme poked her head out of Rachel's pocket and the sun sparkled on her dark, wavy hair. "Let's keep a look out for anything unusual," she said. "We've got to stop Jack Frost and the goblins, or there won't be any ice creams for Treat Day, the day after tomorrow!"

The girls wandered through the market, watching carefully for strange goings-on. One lady selling jewellery had a hood hiding her face. Kirsty stared, wondering if she was a goblin in disguise. Then the lady gave a beaming smile at her customer, and Kirsty glanced away. No – she definitely *wasn't* a goblin. No goblin was ever that nice and friendly!

Next was a stall selling wooden toys and Rachel narrowed her eyes suspiciously when she saw that the stallholder had a baseball cap pulled low over his face. Was *that* a goblin?

Then he lifted his cap and scratched his head, and Rachel saw that his skin was pink and shiny rather than goblin-green. No – he wasn't a goblin either.

"Maybe the ice cream just melted in the sun," Kirsty said doubtfully. "Maybe Charlie's freezer really *had* broken."

Esme shook her head. "No," she said. "I'm sure I can sense goblins around here somewhere. Let's keep looking."

"Hey, Kirsty," came a voice just then, and the girls turned to see two boys approaching.

"Hi Liam, hi Jamal," Kirsty said. "This is my friend Rachel. Liam and Jamal go to my school," she explained.

Rachel said "hi" and then her gaze locked onto the boys' hands. Both were carrying enormous green ice creams!  Jamal licked his, a blissful expression on his face. "These are the nicest ice creams I've ever tasted," he sighed. "The flavours sound really weird, but they taste amazing!"

Rachel and Kirsty exchanged a glance.

"Did you buy them from Charlie?" Kirsty asked, pointing at the van behind them.

"No," Liam replied, "they're from that van over there – the bright green one. All their ice creams are green, too!"

Hidden in Rachel's pocket, Esme gave a squeak of excitement, and both girls knew why. The green ice cream van must surely be connected with the goblins!

"Thanks," said Kirsty. "Come on, Rachel. Let's go there right now!"

A Cool Pool?

There was a long queue stretching back from the green ice cream van, and the girls joined the end. Everyone walking away with their bright green ice creams was exclaiming how delicious they were.

"Look – we were right," whispered Rachel. "Goblins in the van!"

Kirsty and Esme looked over. The three ice cream sellers in the van were dressed in uniforms similar to Charlie's, except they were bright green, and they wore caps over their eyes. But even the caps couldn't disguise what long noses they all had… and how green their skin was!

"One of them must have my magic ice cream cone charm!" said Esme. "Girls, shall we find a quiet place so that I can turn you into fairies? Then we can fly into the van for a closer look without being seen."

"Yes, please," Kirsty said at once.

Being a fairy was always so much fun!

Rachel and Kirsty left the queue and hid behind a van selling cups of tea and coffee. There, Esme waved her wand and murmured some magic words. In the next moment, a swirl of bright stars and sparkles flooded from the wand and whirled around the girls. They immediately shrank smaller and smaller until they were the same size as Esme, and fluttered off the ground with their very own shimmering, gauzy wings.

37

"Thank you!" Rachel cried, twirling in mid-air.

"Let's investigate," Kirsty said, zooming high. "Come on!"

The three fairies flew high above the crowd as they headed for the ice cream

van. The back door was open so they zipped inside and hid on a shelf behind a huge tub of green ice cream. Peeping out, they could see the three goblins working at the counter.

"There you go," said the first goblin to a customer, handing over two cones full of green ice cream and decorated with green fudge sauce. "Who's next?"

"This is the best job ever," the second goblin said. He was making an ice cream sundae, decorated with green whipped cream, and paused to squirt cream into his mouth. "Yum!" he said happily.

"We mustn't use all the ice cream, remember," the third goblin said bossily. "We've got to keep enough back for Jack Frost's Candy Castle."

"That's right – he's going to fill his

swimming pool with ice cream, isn't he?" the first goblin said, adding green sprinkles to another cone. "How cool is that!" He guffawed suddenly. "Cool – ice cream. Do you get it?"

The fairies exchanged glances as the goblins chortled.

"*I* wouldn't want to swim in ice cream," Rachel whispered, shivering. "Think how cold it would be."

"And sticky," Kirsty said, wrinkling her nose.

Esme looked upset. "Ice cream isn't

meant for *swimming* in," she said. "It's for cones and sundaes and milkshakes and knickerbocker glories. What is Jack Frost *thinking*?"

"It's such a waste, too," Rachel agreed. "Especially when the fairies need ice cream for Treat Day. We've got to find your magical charm fast, and stop this nonsense!"

Turning Green

Meanwhile, the goblins had started bickering. "The ice cream pool should be Spinach Swirl flavour," the first goblin said.

"No way – Broccoli Chunk is the best," the second goblin argued, squirting more whipped cream into his mouth.

"You two don't know what you're talking about," the third put in.

"Cabbage Surprise is the tastiest. Imagine diving off the board and landing headfirst in *that*!"

"Diving board? There isn't going to be a diving board," scoffed the first. "I heard Jack Frost was putting one of those super-fast water slides in the pool. It's going to be awesome!"

While the goblins squabbled, Kirsty, Rachel and Esme began quietly searching through the van. It was well

stocked with lots of different flavours
of ice cream (all green) as well as
green hundreds and thousands, green
sauces, green cones,
green cherries
and green
chocolate
flakes.
Searching
through
everything
was nerve-
racking –
especially as the
goblins were so close

and kept turning round to use different
toppings and sauces. Both Kirsty and
Rachel had to move very quickly more
than once, dreading being spotted.

45

Unfortunately, after searching high and low, there was no sign anywhere of Esme's magical ice cream cone charm.

"I don't understand it," Esme sighed, as they fluttered back to the shelf. "We've looked everywhere! Where can it be?"

"Maybe one of the goblins is wearing it on a chain around his neck," Kirsty suggested. So each fairy flew to a different goblin, perched lightly on his  shoulder and peered down his collar. No chains were to be seen, though.

46

"Do they have pockets on their uniforms?" Esme wondered. "Maybe one goblin has the charm hidden in a pocket."

But it only took a moment for them to realise that the goblins didn't have any pockets on their jackets, so the magic charm couldn't be there either.

Just as they were starting to feel stumped, Rachel's eye was caught by the goblins' paper caps, and remembered how Esme had been hiding in one earlier. "Maybe the charm is underneath one of their hats," she whispered. "Although which one?"

Kirsty thought for a moment. "I've got an idea," she said with a smile. "Follow me."

Kirsty flitted out of the back door with Esme and Rachel close behind, and explained her plan.

"The goblins are arguing so much already, I bet we can persuade them to have a food fight with the ice cream.

And then their hats are sure to be knocked off!" she said.

"I love it," Esme said. "But how can we encourage them to have a food fight?"

Rachel grinned. "By starting one ourselves," she suggested. "Could you use your magic, Esme, to disguise us as goblin ice cream sellers? We could set them a very bad example…"

Esme's eyes twinkled. "Perfect," she said. "Although I'll just get rid of this crowd of people first. I would hate any of them to get splattered in the process!"

Esme tapped herself lightly on the head with her wand and murmured a magical enchantment. Then she began to speak... but her words came out much louder than usual. In fact, she sounded exactly like a loudspeaker announcement!

"Ladies and gentlemen," she boomed. "I regret to inform you that the Bright Green Ice Cream Machine has now run out of ice cream, and we are no longer able to serve you. We apologise for any disappointment."

A great sigh of dismay went up from the crowds who had gathered around the van. The goblins, meanwhile, were still arguing so fiercely that they didn't even notice their queue wandering away.

Esme tapped her head again, breaking the enchantment on her voice. "There – now for part two of the plan," she said with a mischievous smile. "Two new ice cream sellers!"

She waved her wand and a flurry of magic sparkles flew around Kirsty and Rachel.

51

The girls grew bigger and greener, with pointy noses and large sticking-out ears.

Rachel giggled at the sight of her and Kirsty now looking so similar to the goblins, with trays of ice cream around their necks. "We definitely look nicer as fairies, rather than goblins," she said.

"I don't feel very dainty any more, with these enormous clumpy feet," Kirsty agreed. "But never mind. We've got a plan to try out. Let's hope it works!"

Splat!

Rachel took a deep breath as she and Kirsty walked out around the front of the van. She knew that Esme's magic wouldn't last long – they only had a few minutes before their goblin disguise wore off. They had to get this right!

Kirsty gave Rachel a wink then launched straight in with her plan.

"You've done it again, haven't you?" she said in a loud, cross voice. "I TOLD you not to keep eating the ice cream. We're meant to be taking it back to Jack Frost, remember?"

"I know that!" Rachel snapped. "And it's not ME who's been eating the ice cream anyway. It must be you!" And with that, she grabbed a scoop of ice cream from a tub left on the counter by a lazy goblin.

The ice cream whizzed through the air, knocking Kirsty's hat off.

"How dare you?" Kirsty cried, pretending to be outraged. "Take THAT!" And she grabbed a nearby stack of cornets and threw them back at Rachel.

As she bent to pick up her fallen hat, Kirsty saw the goblins' faces light up with glee. Goblins could never resist a scrap!

Within moments, they had all joined the food fight – hurling ice cream, sprinkles and cherries at one another. One goblin even used the can of squirty whipped cream like a water pistol, squirting the other goblins in the face.

Rachel and Kirsty grinned. The plan was working! They each grabbed more ice cream and began hurling soft lumps of it into the van.

Splat! One lump knocked off the first goblin's paper hat...but nothing was hidden underneath.

Splat! Kirsty had to aim high as the next goblin was quite tall, but the gooey scoop she threw sent his hat flying too. She held her breath as it fell...but his head was bare beneath it.

Now there was only one goblin left wearing a hat...and Kirsty and Rachel both took careful aim. *Splat! Splat!*

Kirsty's scoop of ice cream just missed, hitting him on the ear, and sliding down his neck. Rachel's scoop, however, was a direct hit, and sent his paper hat flying! There underneath was a small pink and golden ice cream cone charm, sparkling as it lay balanced on the goblin's head.

"Quick, Esme!" hissed Rachel in delight.

Hiding in Rachel's pocket, Esme had seen everything. Out she darted like a bright speck of light, flying straight for the magical charm.

Just as she was about to stretch out and grab it, one of the other goblins noticed her. "Hey! Watch out! There's a sneaky fairy in here!" he cried, batting at Esme with his ice cream scoop.

"She's after the magic cone!" the tall goblin realised. He snatched the charm off the third goblin's head and dashed out of the van at top speed.

Rachel opened her mouth to shout "After him!" but remembered at the last second that she was still disguised as a goblin. Instead, she shouted, "Don't worry, I'll catch that fairy!" and set off after Esme, who was already flying after the tall goblin.

Kirsty joined her. "Come back here!" she yelled. Really, both girls hoped Esme would catch up with the tall goblin but unfortunately he was a fast runner, and showed no sign of slowing down.

"He's getting away," Rachel realised with a groan as they pelted along behind the goblin and Esme.

"And our plan had been working so well!" Kirsty sighed. "Now what are we going to do?"

Trapped!

"The goblin's too fast, I don't think Esme can catch him," Rachel said, "unless he ends up in a dead end somewhere..."

Kirsty grinned. "Wouldn't it be awful if his goblin friends sent him the wrong way?" she said with a wink. "There's an alley just off the main road which is a dead end. Let's try and send him down there."

"Genius!" Rachel smiled, then called ahead to the goblin. "There's a short cut on your left!" she yelled. "You can get away from the fairy if you go that way."

He glanced back, saw Rachel – still disguised as a goblin – and gave her a thumbs-up. Then he ducked down the alley, with Esme, Kirsty and Rachel all following him.

Of course, the alley wasn't a short cut at all – it led to a high brick wall. There was no escape! The goblin wheeled round.

"This isn't a short cut!" he yelled. His eyes widened at the sight of Esme darting towards him. "Now what?"

"Throw the charm to me, I'll look after it!" Rachel called.

Thinking she was a goblin, the tall goblin did as he was told. Rachel deftly caught the charm and held it out on her palm for Esme.

The goblin's jaw dropped as Esme flew down to take it. In the next second, the girls' goblin disguises wore off.

"You tricked me!" the goblin wailed, stamping his foot.

"Of all the rotten cheats!"

The other two goblins had caught up now, panting and clutching their sides. They groaned when they realised what had happened. "And we've used up almost all the ice cream in our food fight," one of them fretted.

"Jack Frost is going to be so angry!"

The goblins looked so worried, the girls felt a bit sorry for them. "It's not your fault that Jack Frost is so greedy," Kirsty said.

"Nobody needs an ice cream swimming pool," Rachel added.

Esme smiled. "Do you think an ice cream *bath* would do instead?" she asked, twirling her wand. In the next second, a large white bath on wheels had appeared... filled with glittering green ice cream!

The goblins looked much more cheerful. "Thank you," they said, and wheeled the bathtub away down the alley.

Esme fastened her magical charm bracelet around her wrist and there was a sudden bright flash of light. "There," she said happily. "Now ice creams everywhere should be super-tasty again."

Rachel grinned. "Well, there's only one way to find out," she said. "Come on, let's pay another visit to Charlie."

The three friends went back down the alley and saw to their delight that Charlie had opened up his ice cream van again and had a large queue of customers waiting eagerly.

"Hooray!" Esme cheered at the sight. "Thank you so much. I'd better go back to Fairyland now to work on my new flavours for Treat Day. Enjoy your ice creams!"

"I'm sure we will," Kirsty said. She and Rachel watched Esme fly away until she was just a tiny dot in the sky, then vanished.

Then the girls joined Charlie's queue. After all their running, they felt quite hungry!

It took a while for Rachel and Kirsty to reach the front of the queue but when it was finally their turn to be served, they noticed two new flavours on the display board. "Ooh, Strawberry Sparkle sounds nice," Kirsty said, opening her purse.

"And I'd like Marshmallow Magic flavour please," Rachel said.

Charlie smiled and handed over their ice creams. Just as he went to serve the next customer, a pinch of glittery hundreds and thousands appeared on their ice creams, and the girls beamed. Fairy magic was so wonderful!

Rachel and Kirsty walked away, licking their ice creams. "Mmm," Rachel said. "Marshmallow Magic is absolutely scrumptious."

"So is Strawberry Sparkle," Kirsty said happily. Then she remembered something. "Oh – and we've still got Aunt Harri's surprise for us back at home, haven't we? I wonder what that might be."

"One thing's for sure," Rachel said as they walked along. "With our Sweet Fairy adventures, we're in for a very tasty time!"

Now it's time for Kirsty and Rachel to help...

Coco the Cupcake Fairy

Read on for a sneak peek...

"This has been such an exciting day,"
said Rachel Walker, licking her
Marshmallow Magic ice cream. "We've
already been to Fairyland and helped
two fairies get their magical objects back
from Jack Frost."

Rachel and her best friend Kirsty
Tate were walking home from the
Wetherbury village square, where they
had been looking around the market.
Rachel was visiting Kirsty for half term,
and it looked as if they were going to
have an exciting holiday.

"The day's not over yet," added Kirsty, smiling.

She paused to lick her Strawberry Sparkle ice cream, which was melting in the hazy afternoon sun and running over her fingers.

"I've got a feeling that now magical things have *started* happening, they're going to keep *on* happening!" she went on, licking her fingers one by one.

No one in the human world knew that the girls had been on many adventures in Fairyland. They were always keen to make new fairy friends, and often they had to help outwit naughty Jack Frost and his troublesome goblin servants. That morning, Honey the Sweet Fairy had visited them to ask for their help. Jack Frost and his goblins had stolen the seven magical objects belonging to the Sweet Fairies. Without them, all the sweets in both the human world and Fairyland were being spoiled.

"We've already rescued Lottie the Lollipop Fairy's magical lollipop charm and Esme the Ice Cream Fairy's magical cone charm," remembered Rachel, chewing on a deliciously sticky marshmallow. "But there are still five more objects to find..."

Read **Coco the Cupcake Fairy** to find out what adventures are in store for Kirsty and Rachel!

Meet the Sweet Fairies

If Kirsty and Rachel don't find the Sweet Fairies' magical charms, Jack Frost will ruin all sweet treats for ever!

www.rainbowmagicbooks.co.uk

RAINBOW magic

Meet the fairies, play games
and get sneak peeks at
the latest books!

www.rainbowmagicbooks.co.uk

There's fairy fun for everyone on
our wonderful website.
You'll find great activities, competitions, stories and
fairy profiles, and also a special newsletter.

Get 30% off all Rainbow Magic books at
www.rainbowmagicbooks.co.uk

Enter the code RAINBOW at the checkout.
Offer ends 31 December 2013.

Offer valid in United Kingdom and Republic of Ireland only.

Competition!

The Sweet Fairies have created a special competition just for you!
In the back of each book in the Sweet Fairies series there will
be a question for you to answer. First you need to collect the
answer from the back of each book in the series.
Once you have all the answers, take the first letter from each one
and arrange them to spell a secret word!
When you have the answer, go online and enter!

We will put all the correct entries into a draw and select a winner
to receive a special Rainbow Magic Goodie Bag featuring lots of
treats for you and your fairy friends. You'll also star in a new
Rainbow Magic story!

Where did Kirsty and Rachel first meet?

_ _ _ _ _ _
_ _ _ _ _

Enter online now at www.rainbowmagicbooks.co.uk

No purchase required. Only one entry per child.
One prize draw will take place on 31st July 2013 and 31st October 2013. Alternatively readers
can send the answer on a postcard to: Rainbow Magic Sweet Fairies Competition,
Orchard Books, 338 Euston Road, London, NW1 3BH. Australian readers can write to:
Rainbow Magic Sweet Fairies Competition, Hachette Children's Books, level 17/207 Kent St,
Sydney, NSW 2000. E-mail: childrens.books@hachette.com.au.
New Zealand readers should write to: Rainbow Magic Sweet Fairies Competition,
4 Whetu Place, Mairangi Bay, Auckland, NZ

Nicki the Holiday Camp Fairy

Rachel and Kirsty have been looking forward to camp, but everything is going wrong. Can they help Nicki fix things, before the whole summer is ruined?

www.rainbowmagicbooks.co.uk